With love to my two-legged
and four-legged family
and friends—S. L. G.

For my little pumpkin,
Dylan Rose—J. W.

BEACH LANE BOOKS
An imprint of Simon & Schuster Children's Publishing Division • 1230 Avenue of the Americas, New York, New
York 10020 • Text copyright © 2017 by Sue Lowell Gallion • Illustrations copyright © 2017 by Joyce Wan • All
rights reserved, including the right of reproduction in whole or in part in any form. • BEACH LANE BOOKS is a
trademark of Simon & Schuster, Inc. • For information about special discounts for bulk purchases, please contact
Simon & Schuster Special Sales at 1-866-506-1949 or business@simonandschuster.com. • The Simon & Schuster
Speakers Bureau can bring authors to your live event. For more information or to book an event, contact the Simon
& Schuster Speakers Bureau at 1-866-248-3049 or visit our website at www.simonspeakers.com. • Book design by
Lauren Rille • The text for this book was set in Baker Street. • The illustrations for this book were rendered in pencil
and then colored digitally. • Manufactured in China • 0517 SCP • First Edition • 10 9 8 7 6 5 4 3 2 1
CIP data for this book is available from the Library of Congress.
ISBN 978-1-4814-4977-9
ISBN 978-1-4814-4978-6 (eBook)

PUG
& PIG
Trick-or-Treat

written by
Sue Lowell Gallion

illustrated by
Joyce Wan

Beach Lane Books • New York London Toronto Sydney New Delhi

This is
Pug and Pig's home.

This is Pug and Pig's scarecrow.

These are Pug and Pig's pumpkins.

And these are Pug and Pig's costumes.

Pig likes the snug fit
of her costume.

She likes how her bones
glow in the dark.

She likes the mask that covers her face.
Will anyone know who she is?

Pig likes her costume very much.

But Pug does not like *his* costume at all.

His insides
feel squished.

His outsides
feel squashed.

He does not like the mask that covers his face.
No one will know who he is!

Pug does not like his costume until . . .

it is scattered all over the yard.

Tonight is Halloween.

This is Pig in costume.

And this is Pug *not*
in costume.
Pug does not care
about Halloween anymore.

But someone else does.

Who will answer the door with Pig?

Who will trick-or-treat with Pig?

Who will go to the Halloween party
and eat tasty tidbits with Pig?

Pug gets an idea.

His idea is in the muddy corner
of the backyard.

Why, who is this?

Perhaps it is Pig's shadow.

Look! Pig answers the door
with her shadow.

Pig goes trick-or-treating
with her shadow.

Pig goes to the Halloween party
and eats tasty tidbits with her shadow.

Pig likes Halloween.

And so does Pug.